HANUKKAH CAT

BY CHAYA BURSTEIN

Illustrated by Judy Hanks–Henn

KAR-BEN COPIES   Rockville, MD

To Ranan, who brought home a wonderful kitten --C.B.
for my family: Jay, Harper Lee, and J.J. -- J.H-H.

Library of Congress Cataloging-in-Publication Data

Burstein, Chaya M.
  Hanukkah cat/ Chaya Burstein; illustrated by Judy
Hanks-Henn.
    p. cm.
    Summary: A hungry cat turns up on Lenny's doorstep
and learns the story of Hanukkah.
ISBN 1-58013-029-1 (pbk.)
  [1. Cats--Fiction. 2. Hanukkah --Fiction.] I. Henn, Judy
Hanks. II. Title.

PZ7.B94553 Han 2001
[E] --dc21

                                    2001029627

Published by Kar-Ben Copies, Inc., 6800 Tildenwood
Lane, Rockville, MD 20852. 1-800-4-KARBEN
Printed in the United States of America

1

On the first night of Hanukkah, an orange kitten tiptoed through Lenny's backyard. She had icicles on her whiskers and snow between her toes, and she was lonely. When she saw the golden light of the Hanukkah candles in Lenny's window, she scrambled to the sill and peeked in.

"Yikes!" yelled Lenny. "There's a green-eyed thing at the window!"

"M-mew..." squeaked the kitten in a shivery voice.

"It's a cat!" cried Lenny. He ran to open the door.

The kitten bounced through the snow and into the house.

"Happy Hanukkah, cat," said Lenny.

"Poor thing. She's cold," said Lenny's mother. She wrapped the kitten in a towel.

"And hungry," said Lenny's father. Quickly he warmed some milk.

Then Lenny held the kitten against his sweater until her orange fur was fluffy-dry and her nose and toes were warm. "Can we keep her? She has no collar. Can she be my Hanukkah present?" he asked.

"Oh, no. A cat is a terrible present," said Lenny's mother. "Cats scratch the furniture and tear the curtains."

"They chase birds and leave hair on the couch and get into all kinds of mischief," Lenny's father added.

"But we can't put her out in the cold," cried Lenny.

"All right," said Lenny's mother. "She can stay until Hanukkah is over."

Lenny fed the cat a potato latke, and they all drank hot cocoa and sang Hanukkah songs. At bedtime, Lenny tucked Hanukkah Cat into a shoebox and kissed her goodnight. "Please try to be good," he whispered. "If you don't tear the curtains or do any of those things, maybe Mommy and Daddy will change their minds."

2

"Mew, mew, meowooo..." yowled Hanukkah Cat early the next morning.

Lenny tumbled out of bed and raced to the kitchen. "Ssshhh," he said. "Be good!" He gave her milk in a saucer and gave himself bread and butter. "Now let's get dressed and go out so we won't wake anybody."

In the yard, Hanukkah Cat nibbled at frozen grass and watched the fat sparrows. Lenny rolled three big snowballs and made a snowman. He put a flower pot on his head and a stick sword in his hand.

"Guess who this is, Hanukkah Cat." he said. Hanukkah Cat padded over and rubbed against Lenny's leg.

Lenny propped the garbage can cover against the snowman. "That's his shield. Now do you know?" he asked. Hanukkah Cat shook the snow from her orange head and trotted up the steps to the front door.

"It's Judah Maccabee. Do you know who he is?"

"Meow," said Hanukkah Cat and stared hopefully at the door.

Lenny came up and tucked the little cat inside his jacket. He could feel her purring against his shirt as he sat down. It tickled.

"I'm going to tell you about Judah Maccabee," he said, "so please don't fall asleep.

"A long time ago, before we were born, the Jewish people lived in the Land of Israel. They had houses and farms and a beautiful Temple where they prayed to God. One day a bad king came and captured their land. He put statues in the Holy Temple and forced the people to bow down and pray to them instead of praying to God.

"Judah Maccabee and some other Jews got very angry. They wouldn't pray to statues. Instead they decided to fight the bad king.

"The king brought in horses and soldiers and big, fighting elephants. But Judah wouldn't give up. He kept fighting until he and his soldiers chased the king's big, strong army right out of the Land of Israel...

"Cat, are you listening?"

Hanukkah Cat wasn't purring anymore. She was curled into a warm ball against his stomach, fast asleep.

"Breakfast," called Lenny's mother.

He stood up slowly, careful not to wake Hanukkah Cat. "Happy dreams," he said. "I'll tell you the rest of the story later."

That night Hanukkah Cat and Lenny and his mother and father lit two Hanukkah candles.

3

Hanukkah Cat loved her new house. It had a soft couch for sharpening her claws. And long, thick curtains for climbing. And a sweet-smelling laundry basket to sleep in. And legs to attack.

"Ouch! Stop that, silly cat. You tore my socks," yelled Lenny's mother.

Hanukkah Cat scooted across the floor and flew into the laundry basket.

"Lenny, this cat has got to go!"

"You promised she could stay," Lenny protested.

"Only until Hanukkah is over. Then out she goes!"

Lenny plucked Hanukkah Cat out of the laundry basket. "Don't worry," he said, "we still have 1, 2, 3, 4, 5, 6 more days. Hanukkah lasts 8 days. Do you know why?"

Hanukkah Cat wiggled and tried to jump down. She wanted to play. But Lenny held her tightly. "Don't make any more trouble! Listen, and I'll tell you the rest of the Hanukkah story.

"Remember I told you how Judah Maccabee and his army chased the king's soldiers out of the Land of Israel? Well, after that, Judah and the other Jews went to the Temple. They threw out the king's statues and scrubbed and painted until everything was shiny clean and beautiful again. Then it was time to light the big, golden menorah. But the priests could find only a little bit of oil — enough to last for only one day."

Hanukkah Cat settled down and started licking Lenny's finger with her rough, pink tongue.

"Cat, listen. This part is very important." Lenny tapped Hanukkah Cat's nose. "The priests poured the little bit of oil into the menorah and lit it. Instead of burning for one day, it burned and burned for eight whole days. And that's why we have Hanukkah for eight days."

He scratched her neck. "I wish the menorah had burned for 100 days," he said. "Then you could stay and stay and stay."

That night they lit three Hanukkah candles.

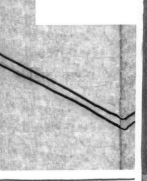

4

Judah the snowman was melting. His sword lay on the ground and a fat blue bird sat on his flower pot hat. Hanukkah Cat poked and sniffed in the snow at his feet.

"Kraaaa!" screeched the blue bird.

Hanukkah Cat looked up and licked her lips. Birds made her hungry.

The blue bird zoomed right past her ear and up to a tree branch. Hanukkah Cat flattened her belly against the snow and watched. Then she jumped and scrambled up the trunk of the tree.

Where was the bird?

Hanukkah Cat climbed higher...

No bird.

...and higher.

The bird was gone.

She started down. But down was far, far away. She slipped and slid and grabbed. "Meow," called Hanukkah Cat. "MEOW!"

Lenny climbed the tree, but he couldn't reach her. His mother got the ladder and climbed high, but Hanukkah Cat was even higher.

"Meow, meowwwwrrr!" she cried.

His father climbed higher and nearly, nearly got her, but Hanukkah Cat slid to the very end of the branch. He reached over to catch her, and CRACK — a ladder rung broke! The ladder fell down. Lenny's father and Hanukkah Cat were hanging side by side.

"Help! Call the fire department!" yelled Lenny's father.

The ladder truck came clanging. The firemen jumped down, raised their ladder, and rushed up just as Hanukkah Cat fell..."Meow!"...right into their arms.

Lenny's father climbed down the ladder. Lenny hugged Hanukkah
Cat and his father and the firemen. He watched as the firemen took
down their ladder, jumped on the truck, and clanged away.

Then it was time to light four Hanukkah candles.

5

Lenny put on his new jeans and sneakers. He tied a ribbon around Hanukkah Cat's neck. Lenny's cousins and their dog Ricky were coming to celebrate the fifth night of Hanukkah.

They ate latkes and applesauce and jelly doughnuts. Then Lenny played dreidel with his cousins. Ricky napped under the couch, with one eye on Hanukkah Cat.

Everybody got a handful of pennies. Lenny spun the dreidel. Hanukkah Cat watched with sparkling eyes.

"*Shin!* Put in a penny," yelled noisy cousin Harry.

Cousin Beth spun next.

"*Nun!*" laughed Harry. "You don't get anything!"

Lenny spun next.

"A *hey!*" yelped Harry. "You take half the pennies."

Hanukkah Cat crouched low.

"Now watch me. I'm going to get a *gimmel* and take all the pennies," crowed Harry. He spun the dreidel. Hanukkah Cat sprang out and grabbed it just as Harry yelled, "*Gimmel!*"

"It was NOT!" yelled Lenny.

"It was TOO!" Harry shouted. "Drop that dreidel. Bad cat!"

Ricky's ears perked up. "Grrr..." he growled.

Hanukkah Cat dropped the dreidel and spun around. Her tail stood straight up, her back arched, and she hissed.

"Arf, arf," Ricky yipped. He scrambled out from under the couch.

Hanukkah Cat sprang up the living room drapes, onto the dining room table...and right through Grandma's apple cake.

"Arf, arf," Ricky barked again, and ran between Lenny's mother's legs. The plate of latkes she was carrying flew out of her hands.

Hanukkah Cat leaped to the sideboard, across the hall, into the kitchen, and landed—SPLUSH— in a sinkful of soapy water.

"Yeow! Spltchhh!"

"Arf! Arf!"

Cousin Harry grabbed Ricky. Lenny rescued Hanukkah Cat. Everyone cheered. "Thank goodness we're only keeping that kitten a few more days," Lenny's mother said.

Then all the cousins took turns lighting five Hanukkah candles.

6

Hanukkah Cat's nose was tickly with feathers and her mouth was full. She had a Hanukkah present for her new family. Pat, pat, pat, she went through the mushy snow right up to the front door. She scratched, but the door didn't open.

Hanukkah Cat heard the swish of the broom in the kitchen.

"Mmmmeeee, mmmmeee," she called proudly without opening her mouth.

Footsteps came clacking through the kitchen. The door opened. "Come on in, cat," said Lenny's mother.

Hanukkah Cat raised her chin to show off the present she had in her mouth.

"Oh! What's that?" Mother's voice had a funny, screechy sound. "A bird! Drop it! Drop that bird!"

BAM! The broom whacked down on Hanukkah Cat's tail.

"Yeow!" she yowled, opening her mouth wide. The bird flopped out. It spread its wings and whirred away over the snow.

"Bad cat! Bad cat!" The broom whacked again.

Hanukkah Cat tumbled down the steps and raced across the yard. She ran under the fence and deep into the black bushes.

Her nose was freezing, but she didn't come out until Lenny called. "Come home, Hanukkah Cat. It's time to light the candles."

Only two more nights, thought Lenny as they lit six candles. And Hanukkah Cat is doing everything wrong. What will happen to her? He looked sadly into the yellow flames. What would Judah Maccabee do if his best friend was in danger, he wondered. Judah would do something BRAVE!

Suddenly, Lenny had an idea.

7

The next morning Lenny told Hanukkah Cat, "I'm not supposed to go off the block, but this is an emergency. We're going to find you a new family, even if we have to walk to...the Land of Israel!" He sat the kitten on his wagon, walked down the block, and bravely crossed the street.

He stopped and knocked at a friendly-looking red house. One old man and six cats answered the door.

"Would you like a kitten?" asked Lenny.

"Do I look like I'd like a kitten?" said the man and closed the door.

He tried a sleepy, shuttered, yellow house next. A lady in a bathrobe answered and said, "No thank you. With three canaries and a parakeet, I certainly don't need a cat."

"This cat loves birds," said Lenny. But the lady had already closed the door.

They started up the walk to the next house, past a tall green fence. A spotted dog, bigger than Lenny, bounded out of the bushes and crashed against the fence, barking and snapping at them.

"Yeow!" screeched Hanukkah Cat, and "Yikes!" yelled Lenny, as they raced away.

They tried a grocery store. But the grocer already had a fine mouser. On the next block they tried a house or two, but nobody wanted a kitten.

Lenny wasn't feeling brave like Judah Maccabee anymore. He was hungry and tired. "I'm sorry, Hanukkah Cat," he said. "We'd better just go home."

But which way was home? Lenny looked up the block and down the block. All the snowy houses looked the same.

Hanukkah Cat was hungry, too. She sniffed the air and wiggled her whiskers. Then she jumped off the wagon and pattered across the street.

"Come back," yelled Lenny. But she pattered even faster.

Lenny looked both ways for cars and then ran across. "Stop! You'll get lost!" he yelled. But Hanukkah Cat ran past the grocery store and scrambled under the bushes into the next yard. Lenny crashed through the bushes close behind. The cat jumped to the top of a green fence and plopped down into a another yard. Huffing and puffing, Lenny made it over the fence.

Suddenly he heard barking. A moment later, the big, spotted dog
came charging around the corner.

Lenny froze. Hanukkah Cat stopped too. She raised her tail, arched
her back, and hissed.

"Grr...row! Ruff, ruff!" the dog thundered.

A small, orange ball suddenly flew at his soft, black nose and dug in
with the needle-sharp claws.

"YI!" the dog yowled. He shook his head and spun around and around. Hanukkah Cat bounced off, and the dog raced away, yipping and yelping. Then Hanukkah Cat and Lenny leaped over the fence and ran as fast as they could, through more backyards, under more fences and, finally, right up their own front steps.

"What a smart cat," said Lenny's mother, when she heard how Hanukkah Cat had led Lenny home.

"And a brave one," said Lenny's father. "She's a real Hanukkah heroine."

They gave her a big bowl of chopped liver, and then they all lit seven Hanukkah candles.

8

It was the last night of Hanukkah. Eight candles and the shamash burned brightly on the window sill. Three packages wrapped in Hanukkah paper sat beside the menorah.

But Lenny didn't care about the packages. This is Hanukkah Cat's last night, he thought sadly.

"Open your presents, Lenny," said his mother.

"I don't feel like it," he answered.

"You'll be surprised," said his father. "Please open them."

"Oh, all right," Lenny said. He pulled the ribbon off the biggest one. Hanukkah Cat grabbed the ribbon and skittered across the floor.

"What kind of toy is this?" asked Lenny.

"Mew!" cried Hanukkah Cat happily. She dropped the ribbon and raced back, right up to the furry top of the new toy.

"It's a scratching post," said Lenny's mother. "Now maybe Hanukkah Cat won't scratch the couch anymore."

"But, Mommy…" Lenny started to say. Then he stopped and opened the smallest package. Bells jingled loudly on a kitten-sized collar.

"Put it on Hanukkah Cat," said his father. "The birds will hear her bells and they'll fly away before she can catch them."

"Daddy, why…" Lenny started to ask, but then he stopped and opened the last package. It was a big oval basket with a soft, blue pillow. "A basket? Why…"

"Hanukkah Cat will have her own basket to sleep in, instead of the laundry basket," his mother said.

"But…why are we giving these presents to Hanukkah Cat?" asked Lenny. "And where is my present?"

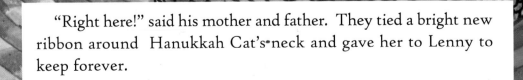

"Right here!" said his mother and father. They tied a bright new ribbon around Hanukkah Cat's neck and gave her to Lenny to keep forever.